Rabén & Sjögren Stockholm

English translation copyright © 1978
by Methuen Children's Books Ltd., London
All rights reserved
First published in 1977 by Follett in the United States of America
Illustrations copyright © 1977 by Ilon Wikland
Originally published in Sweden by Rabén & Sjögren
under the title *Visst kan Lotta nästan allting,*
text copyright © 1977 by Astrid Lindgren
Library of Congress catalog card number: 90-60542
Printed in Denmark
This edition first published in 1990
ISBN 91 29 59782 X

R&S Books are distributed in the United States of America
by Farrar, Straus and Giroux, New York;
in the United Kingdom by Ragged Bears, Andover;
in Canada by Vanwell Publishing, St. Catharines,
and in Australia by ERA Publications, Adelaide

Astrid Lindgren

LOTTA'S CHRISTMAS SURPRISE

Illustrated by
Ilon Wikland

R&S
BOOKS

Stockholm   New York   London   Adelaide   Toronto

"It's funny," said Lotta, "how many things I can do." She had just let Jonas and Maria hear how well she could whistle, so no wonder she was pleased.

"Come to think of it, I can do anything," she said.

"You certainly know how to brag," said Maria.

Jonas was silent for a moment. "What about slalom skiing?" He just said that because he was learning how to do it

himself.

It made Lotta angry. "Did I say I could slalom?" she said.

"You said you could do anything," said Jonas.

"And I can, too," said Lotta. "Anything except slalom."

"Okay, okay," said Jonas. And then he and Maria left for the big ski slope with their skis. Lotta wanted to go skiing, too. But not on the big slope.

I can ski right here in the yard and learn to slalom, too, she thought. It can't be hard. First you go in one direction and then in the other direction, and all the time you wobble your bottom. Anyway, I can wobble my bottom already, she thought, trying it to see how good she was.

But before she did any difficult skiing, she went to see if her mother had anything for her to do. In the kitchen, in the yellow house where they lived, Lotta's mother was busy with her Christmas baking. She decorated and kneaded and rushed around in a great hurry.

She smiled when she saw Lotta. "Lotta, can you take this Christmas bread to Mrs. Berg?" she said. "And see if you can do anything to help her."

Lotta was happy to go see Mrs. Berg. "Of course, I can do that, too. Help people who are sick. I can do anything — almost!"

Mrs. Berg lived next door, and she wasn't feeling well. Lotta knew she was always out of breath.

"I'm taking Teddy with me to help cheer up Mrs. Berg," said Lotta. Teddy was an old stuffed pig made of cloth. Lotta had had him since she was little, and she still dragged him around everywhere, even though she was a big girl now, over five, in fact.

Mom put the bread into a plastic bag and fastened it with a rubber band. "Say hello to Mrs. Berg for me," she said, and gave Lotta the bag. "Come to think of it, you can take out the garbage at the same time."

"Just give it to me," said Lotta. "I'll take care of everything."

Lotta's mother tied up the garbage with a rubber band, too. Lying on top was a fish head. They had had pike for dinner the night before, and the fish stared at Lotta through the plastic with horrible white eyes.

"Disgusting," said Lotta, holding out the bag so Teddy could see it, too. "There's a monster in this bag," she told him. "But now it's going into the garbage!" Then Lotta went out with a bag in each hand and Teddy under her arm.

Outside the kitchen door were her skis. I'll learn to slalom, thought Lotta, if possible, before Jonas and Maria come home.

"We can slalom over to Mrs. Berg's," she said to Teddy, stepping into her skis. But Lotta was not used to skiing with two plastic bags *and* Teddy.

"It won't work," she said to Teddy. "I'll have to stuff you in the bread bag." She squeezed him into the bag and fastened it with the rubber band. She was sure his eyes were looking sadly at her through the plastic.

"It'll only take a minute," Lotta said. "And if you get hungry, you can nibble on the bread. Just make sure it can't be seen."

Then she showed Teddy how to slalom ski.

"First in one direction," she said, swinging around the apple tree. "And then in the other direction," she said, setting off toward the cherry tree. She wobbled her bottom, too, when she remembered to. Sometimes she forgot, but it seemed to work anyway.

Lotta was going very fast. There was a little slope going down to the garbage can, and Lotta slowed down just in time to toss the bag in. Then she raced on. Lotta was out of breath when she reached Mrs. Berg's. But not as much as Mrs. Berg herself.

Mrs. Berg was in bed, propped up on her pillow, breathing heavily.

"How's your out-of-breathness?" said Lotta. Mrs Berg said it was a little better.

"Lucky for you I came," said Lotta. "Guess what I brought you."

She held the bag behind her back so Mrs. Berg couldn't see it. "I wonder what it could be," said Mrs. Berg.

"It's something to eat. It begins with LO, but I'm not saying what it is. You could also say it begins with B . . . RRR," said Lotta, giving Mrs. Berg another clue.

"LO and B . . . RRR," said Mrs. Berg. "No, I can't guess."

"You can cut it in slices and spread butter on it," said Lotta. "I'm not telling you anything else. Come on, guess!"

"LO . . . is it a loaf?" asked Mrs. Berg. Lotta laughed.

"Right! And BRRR, that means bread, see?" She held out the bag. But then she screamed. There was no bread in it!

"You horrible monster," she shouted, as she saw the fish eyes staring at her through the plastic.

"You haven't brought me a monster, have you?" asked Mrs. Berg in a very surprised voice. But Lotta was already halfway out the door. Where was Teddy? And Mrs. Berg's bread? In the garbage, of course. She ran all the way back with a lump in her throat, because she knew just how horrible Teddy must be feeling down there in the dark, all alone.

"Poor Teddy," she said, lifting the garbage-can lid. Then Lotta screamed so loud that everyone on the street must have heard her. It was empty. There was no Teddy and no bread! Of course, it was Friday. On Fridays, Charlie Fry came with his garbage truck.

"My Teddy," yelled Lotta, running down the street.

The garbage truck was standing next to Larsson's Bakery. Charlie Fry was shoving Larsson's garbage bag into the huge open mouth at the back of the truck. Lotta knew there was a kind of mill in the back which ground up all the garbage into one big, pulpy mass. Charlie Fry had shown her once.

Lotta screamed. She knew that was the end of Teddy. He was just a pulpy mass now and not her Teddy. And it was all her fault!

"What are you yelling about?" said Charlie.

"My Teddy!" screamed Lotta. "You've ground him to pieces!"

Charlie was almost as sad as Lotta when he realized what had happened. And Lotta just went on screaming.

"My Teddy! My Teddy!" shouted Lotta. Then she stared angrily at Charlie, even though it wasn't his fault at all.

"You've ground up Mrs. Berg's bread, too," yelled Lotta.

"Bread?" said Charlie. "Was it in a plastic bag?"

"Yes, and Teddy, too," screamed Lotta. "And now he's dead."

"But I put that bag aside," said Charlie. "I need bread for my birds."

Lotta stopped crying, and Charlie went to get the bag. What if it wasn't the right one?

But it was.

"I didn't see any Teddy in it," said Charlie.

"Didn't you see him with that sad look in his eyes?" said Lotta. She tore Teddy out of the bag and hugged him, saying, "Forgive me, forgive me," over and over again.

Suddenly she saw the bag that she had thrown on the ground, the one with the monster in it. With a yell she grabbed it and threw it right into the mouth of the garbage truck.

"Now you'll be a squashed monster," she said. "And that suits me fine!"

Then Lotta went back to Mrs. Berg's with Teddy in one hand and the bread in the other.

"I'm never going to learn to slalom," she said. "That's what caused all this trouble in the first place."

"Did you leave the bread somewhere?" said Mrs. Berg when Lotta returned.

"Oh, no," said Lotta. "It's just been on a little trip with my Teddy."

Mrs. Berg kept Teddy in bed with her while Lotta showed her how good she was at everything. Lotta watered all Mrs. Berg's plants, and Scotty, Mrs. Berg's snappy little dog, got watered a bit, too. And, of course, he barked at Lotta the whole time. Lotta shook out Mrs. Berg's pillows to make them nice and fluffy, and she cut some slices of the bread and buttered them. She made Mrs. Berg eat them because it was good for her out-of-breathness. She washed a few dishes, swept the floor, and even she was amazed at how well she could do everything.

"Of course, it's a lot of hard work," said Lotta. "Is there anything else you want me to do?"

"Yes, dear. Would you mind running down to the newsstand to buy me a paper?" said Mrs. Berg. Lotta was quite happy to do that.

"They've got really good candy there," she told Mrs. Berg. Mrs. Berg gave her money for the newspaper and Lotta got a little extra change for being such a big help.

"I have to go home for a minute first," she said, "because I want to see the Christmas tree. Dad said he'd have it with him when he came home for lunch."

But when Lotta walked into the kitchen, she was just in time to hear her father's awful news.

"There's not a Christmas tree for sale in the whole town," he said.

Mom was busy making pancakes. "No Christmas tree," she said. "What do you mean? Of course, there must be a Christmas tree for sale." But Lotta's father meant exactly what he said. The Christmas trees were all sold out.

Jonas and Maria and Lotta didn't want to believe it.

"We have to have a Christmas tree," said Jonas.

"Have to, have to. I'm not a magician," said Dad. "I can't do everything."

"But you could have bought one before," said Maria. "Why didn't you?"

Dad explained that he always bought the Christmas tree in the big square three days before Christmas. And usually there were plenty of trees. But this year all the snow had made it hard to bring in enough trees from the forest. In any case, there was none left in the square, and there was nothing he could do.

Jonas looked at Lotta. "You said you could do anything, Lotta," he said, "so get us a Christmas tree."

"Time to eat," said Mom.

They had their pancakes in silence, feeling very sad. A Christmas without a Christmas tree. That just wasn't right.

Then Dad had to go back to work. "I'll search the whole town," he said. "If there's a tree to be had, I'll get it. But if there isn't, then there just isn't."

Jonas and Maria cried. But before Lotta could cry too, she had to go to the newsstand to buy a paper for Mrs. Berg.

"You can come along," she said to Teddy. "We'll take the sled and have some fun, even though we're all miserable."

It was downhill all the way to the newsstand.
"Look out below!" shouted Lotta, and she was
off.

Lotta had to pull the sled the last little bit because the newsstand was beside the gas station, and the gas station was just off a big main road, where she couldn't go on her sled.

Mr. Bloomfield was in charge of the gas station, and his wife looked after the shop.

"Hello, little Lotta," said Mrs. Bloomfield. "How are things today?"

"Awful," said Lotta. "We're not going to have a Christmas tree this year."

"That's very sad," said Mrs. Bloomfield. "I heard that all the Christmas trees in town are gone."

"Yes," said Lotta. "I'm going to cry when I get home."

But first she bought a paper for Mrs. Berg and then she stood and thought about what kind of candy to buy. These things just couldn't be decided in a hurry.

While Lotta was thinking, something incredible happened. A huge truck came thundering into the gas station, and this particular truck — believe it or not — was loaded with Christmas trees, so high that they had to be piled on top of each other. Lotta became very excited.

This was no time to think about candy. How lucky she hadn't had time to spend her money. Surely a Christmas tree couldn't cost that much.

She rushed over to the driver, who was busy filling his tank.

"Can I buy a Christmas tree?" she asked. But the driver didn't even look at Lotta. "No, you can't," he said grumpily.

"Why?" asked Lotta.

"They are going to the big city, every last one of them," said the driver.

"Why?" asked Lotta.

"Why, why, because they haven't got any Christmas trees there."

"We haven't got any here, either," said Lotta.

"But in the city they'll pay anything for them. Now, out of my way," said the driver,

going in to pay Mrs. Bloomfield for the gas.

Lotta ran after him. "I'll pay anything, too," she shouted, with tears in her eyes. "You can give me a little tree, can't you?"

"That's what you think! Now out of my way," said the driver. He didn't want Lotta bothering him. When he had paid, he went straight over to his truck, ready to drive off.

Lotta ran after him.

"Please, please," she screamed, holding up her money.

"Bye, bye, kid," said the driver, banging the door shut. And then he drove off.

Lotta cried; she couldn't wait till she got home. It was horrible. A load of Christmas trees, and she couldn't have even one. She hated that driver. She glared after him. He had to make a big turn to get out on the road, and he was driving much too fast. Even Lotta could see that.

Then something strange happened. As the truck raced around the corner, one of the trees rolled off the load and landed on the side of the road.

"You dropped a tree," shouted Lotta. She was always helpful. But the driver neither heard nor saw her. He just drove on. And there stood Lotta. Watching the taillights getting smaller and smaller.

Just then Mr. Bloomfield came out.

"Look, there's a tree lying over there," said Lotta. "And I need it. Do you think I can take it?"

"Well, why not?" said Mr. Bloomfield. "It can't just lie there."

"Well, I never," said Mrs. Bloomfield from the newsstand. "Just your luck, Lotta."

"But what if the driver comes back?" said Lotta uneasily.

"He'll have only himself to blame," said Mrs. Bloomfield. "He shouldn't have been throwing his trees around in the first place."

Lotta thought for a moment. "Do you want to take my money, just in case? If he comes back, you can pay him."

"Okay," said Mr. Bloomfield. "And if we don't hear from him, you'll get your money back after Christmas."

It was a large and beautiful tree. Much too big for Lotta. But Mr. Bloomfield helped her tie it to the sled.

Lotta arranged a seat for Teddy. "It'll be the best ride you've ever had," she said.

"Bye and thanks," said Lotta. She whistled all the way home.

"Now that's what I call a good whistle," she said to Teddy.

When she walked into the kitchen, she looked very secretive. But nobody noticed. Jonas and Maria sat in their chairs, crying, and Mom was busy comforting them. No one looked at Lotta.

"What are you two crying about?" said Lotta.

"Dad called," said Mom. "There's not one tree in the whole town."

"That's strange," said Lotta. "Come see what I've got on my sled."

But Jonas and Maria just went on crying and didn't hear a word Lotta said.

"What kind of Christmas will this be," said Maria, "without a tree!"

"Come and see what I've got on my sled," said Lotta again.

"Stop pestering us, Lotta," said Jonas.

"We don't want to look at anything. We're too busy crying."

"Too bad," said Lotta. "You could have seen a Christmas tree."

"Now you're lying again," said Maria. But they rushed outside with Mom.

In front of the kitchen door stood Lotta's sled, and on it was the most beautiful Christmas tree imaginable. Teddy was sitting on a branch, looking as if he'd brought the whole load himself. Jonas and Maria just stared. And Mom said: "But, Lotta, where in the world did you get it?"

"Guess," said Lotta.

Then Jonas threw his arms around her. "You were right, Lotta. You really can do anything."

"Didn't I tell you?" said Lotta.

The night before Christmas Eve was tree-decorating night in the yellow house. Everyone helped. Dad and Mom and Jonas and Maria and Lotta. And for the tenth time Lotta told the story of the truck and the driver.

"We've never had such a nice tree," said Maria. "Look what beautiful pine needles it's got!"

"And what a good smell," said Jonas.

"This is something we'll never forget," said Mom. "Imagine, coming home with a Christmas tree for us."

"We'll remember the Lotta tree when all the other trees are forgotten," said Dad.

Lotta said nothing. She just thought: It's strange, there are so many things I can do. Find Christmas trees and just about anything. Then she looked lovingly at Teddy, who was standing under the tree on his crooked little legs.

"Yes, anything," she said. "Except ski with two bags *and* Teddy!"